T 7949

*17571*

D0437393

# A NOTE TO PARENTS

### Reading Aloud with Your Child

*Research shows that reading books aloud is the single most valuable support parents can provide in helping children learn to read.*

- Be a ham! The more enthusiasm you display, the more your child will enjoy the book.
- Run your finger underneath the words as you read to signal that the print carries the story.
- Leave time for examining the illustrations more closely; encourage your child to find things in the pictures.
- Invite your youngster to join in whenever there's a repeated phrase in the text.
- Link up events in the book with similar events in your child's life.
- If your child asks a question, stop and answer it. The book can be a means to learning more about your child's thoughts.

### Listening to Your Child Read Aloud

*The support of your attention and praise is absolutely crucial to your child's continuing efforts to learn to read.*

- If your child is learning to read and asks for a word, give it immediately so that the meaning of the story is not interrupted. DO NOT ask your child to sound out the word.
- On the other hand, if your child initiates the act of sounding out, don't intervene.
- If your child is reading along and makes what is called a miscue, listen for the sense of the miscue. If the word "road" is substituted for the word "street," for instance, no meaning is lost. Don't stop the reading for a correction.
- If the miscue makes no sense (for example, "horse" for "house"), ask your child to reread the sentence because you're not sure you understand what's just been read.
- Above all else, enjoy your child's growing command of print and make sure you give lots of praise. *You are your child's first teacher — and the most important one. Praise from you is critical for further risk-taking and learning.*

— Priscilla Lynch
Ph.D., New York University
Educational Consultant

*For John*
*—D.M.*

ISBN 0-590-73887-9

Copyright © 1997 by David McPhail.
All rights reserved. Published by Scholastic Inc.
HELLO READER!, CARTWHEEL BOOKS, and the CARTWHEEL BOOKS logo are registered trademarks of Scholastic Inc.

Library of Congress Cataloging-in-Publication Data available.

12 11 10 9 8 7 6 5 4 3 2          7 8 9/9 0 1 2/0

Printed in the U.S.A.                              24

First Scholastic printing, February 1997

1 7 5 7 1

# The Day the Dog Said, "Cock·a·Doodle·Doo!"

by David McPhail

**Hello Reader! — Level 2**

SCHOLASTIC INC.
New York Toronto London Auckland Sydney

# One sunny day,
the animals were talking.

"It's hot,"
said the duck.
"Quack!"

"Very,"
said the goose.
"Honk!"

"Moo!
Maybe it will rain,"
said the cow.

"I hope so," said the pig,
whose mud puddle was drying up.
"Oink!"

"Rain brings out the best worms,"
said the rooster.
"Cock-a-doodle-doo!"

The dog barked at the rooster.
"Stop that!
I'm trying to sleep! Woof!"

"I can't help it," said the rooster.
"I'm a rooster, and roosters say
cock-a-doodle-doo!"

Just then,
a strong wind blew
through the barnyard.
It stirred up a cloud of dust
and sent the animals
tumbling through the air.

Then it stopped.

"Is everyone all right?"
asked the duck.
"Moo!"

"I'm okay,"
said the goose.
"Oink!"

"Me, too," said the cow. "Quack!"

"Same here," said the pig. "Honk!"

"I lost a few tail feathers," said the rooster. "Woof!"

Said the dog to the rooster, "I like that sound. Cock-a-doodle-doo!"

"And I like *your* sound," the rooster told the dog.

"Well, I think that the duck sounds *lovely*," said the cow.

"The goose sounds even better," said the pig.

"The cow sounds best of all!" said the duck.

"The pig is best!" said the goose.

The animals were so busy arguing
that they didn't notice
the sky grow dark.

Then, as before, a strong wind
blew through the barnyard,
stirred up a cloud of dust,
and sent the animals flying.

When the wind stopped,
a gentle rain began to fall.

No one said a word.

Then the duck spoke.
"I guess I'll go for a swim,"
he said. "Quack!"

"Wait for me," said the goose.
"Honk!"

"Moo," said the cow.
"I'm moving to the pasture
to eat some grass."

The pig jumped into a new mud
puddle with a happy "Oink!"

"As for me," said the rooster,
"I've been invited to a party
at the henhouse. See you later.
Cock-a-doodle-doo!"

"Woof!" said the dog.
"It's time for a nap."

Then the barnyard was quiet—
except for the patter of raindrops,
the chatter of hens...

and the sound of a snoring dog.